Norman and Brenda

Colin Thompson & Amy Lissiat

Kane/Miller
BOOK PUBLISHERS

Norman felt as if life had started without him. Everyone else was having theirs, but his hadn't arrived yet.

This wasn't a new feeling. He'd always had it, from his earliest memory right up until now, his thirty-seventh birthday.

Brenda felt as if life was always going on in the next room. If she went into the next room, it moved out into the garden.

It wasn't a new feeling, but as the years passed it got stronger and stronger until by the time she was thirty-seven it was all she could think of.

Everyone else had stuff that made them laugh and cry, but Norman just seemed to have a straight line. He was never sad, but then he was never really happy either. Other people fell in and out of love. Norman only fell on the path and grazed his knee.

Everyone else had other stuff in their heads, stuff that made them fall in and out of love. Brenda only fell into the flowerbed and squashed the chrysanthemums.

She was the sort of person who ended up in the kitchen at parties doing the washing up and saying, "No, no, I don't mind at all. Where do the fish knives go?

After his thirtieth birthday, people said, "Oh, that's just old Norman."

Norman thought thirty was too young to be called old, but on reflectio
he could see they were right. He had been born old.

After her thirtieth birthday Brenda stopped going to parties
because her hands were losing their softness and taking your
own rubber gloves to parties was not the thing to do.

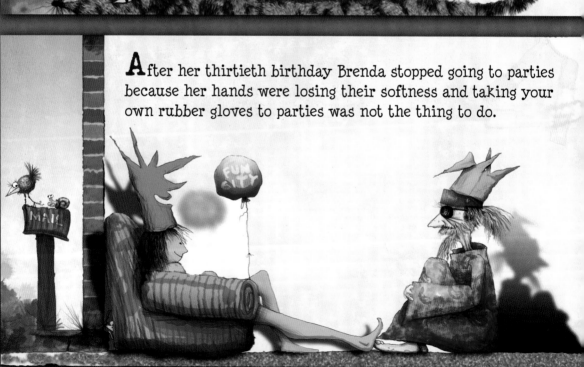

Sometimes a cloud would fall in love with Norman and follow him around, raining on him until it ran out of water. This could take several days. When Norman went indoors the cloud would hover over the house until he came out again. Once Norman tried to get away by going out the back door, but the cloud found him and rained on him extra hard to punish him.

Puddles were deeply attracted to Brenda and would go out of their way to climb inside her shoes, even when she wore her waterproof boots. She tried staying indoors when it was raining, but her water pipes burst and filled not only the shoes she was wearing but all the other pairs in her closet.

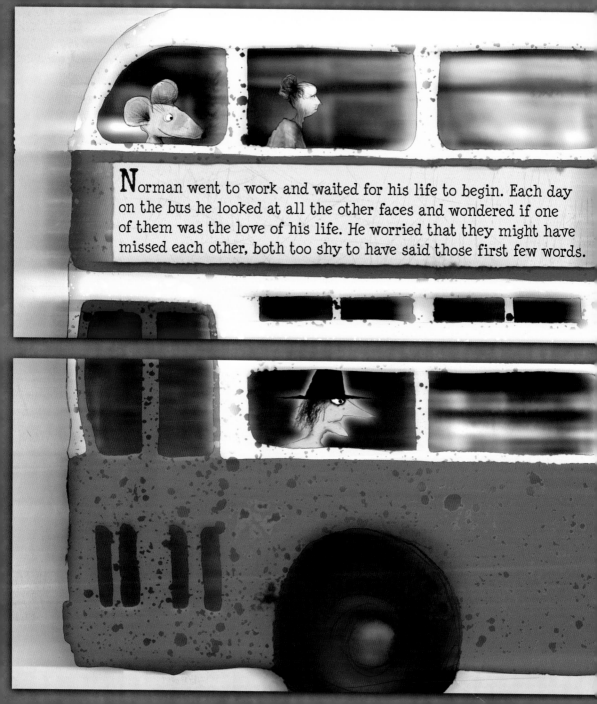

Norman went to work and waited for his life to begin. Each day on the bus he looked at all the other faces and wondered if one of them was the love of his life. He worried that they might have missed each other, both too shy to have said those first few words.

27 WORK
Drudgery

When Brenda went to work on the bus each day she looked at all the other faces and wondered if one of them was the love of her life. She worried that they might have missed each other, but if anyone ever did look back, she stared into her handbag.

He bought a goldfish and in the long evenings, Norman and Fiona sat and stared at each other, but goldfish have fickle hearts and short memories and every time Norman went to the bathroom, Fiona forgot him. Norman soon realized that recreating the relationship several times an evening — Norman drank a lot of coffee and went to the bathroom at least four times between dinner and bedtime — was leading nowhere, so he gave Fiona to the children next door. They weren't grateful and always avoided him after that.

She bought an axolotl and in the long evenings, Brenda and Spartacus sat and stared at each other, but axolotls are capricious and one night while Brenda was in the bath, Spartacus changed into a salamander, climbed out of his tank and ran away.

Norman became thirty-eight and then thirty-nine and still his life didn't begin. In fact, there were times when he felt it was all going backwards. His hair deserted him. Some of it moved down his body to his back, but most of it tried to escape by falling on the floor and hiding in the vacuum cleaner. Several of his teeth went too.

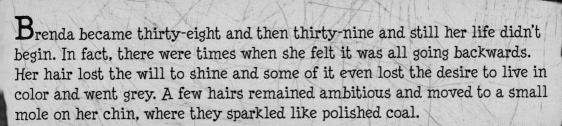

Brenda became thirty-eight and then thirty-nine and still her life didn't begin. In fact, there were times when she felt it was all going backwards. Her hair lost the will to shine and some of it even lost the desire to live in color and went grey. A few hairs remained ambitious and moved to a small mole on her chin, where they sparkled like polished coal.

When he was forty, Norman thought that he had finally reached an age where he could stop worrying about life, but he hadn't. He still wondered if every passing face was the love of his life, or if he would turn a corner into a new place where fulfillment and deep meaning were waiting for him.

He wouldn't have minded if his life was only half-filled with only a bit of shallow meaning, but even that eluded him.

When she was forty, Brenda thought that she had finally reached an age where she could stop worrying about life, but she hadn't. She still wondered if every skirt made her bottom look too big, or if the love of her life would ride up on a white horse and whisk her away.

She wouldn't have minded if he rode up on a bicycle but the only thing that rode up was her underwear.

Norman had no one to talk to, so he bought a budgie and called it George. George laid an egg and spent all day ignoring Norman and talking to her reflection. George's reflection was more animated than Norman. The relationship was going nowhere so Norman gave George to the children across the street, who refused her. They were friends of the children next door.

Norman thought about giving George her freedom, but in the end he gave her to an old people's home where she never stopped talking.

To make herself feel better, Brenda began visiting the old people's home. All the people there were far worse off than she was. At least she didn't dribble or talk to the wall or go to the toilet before she got to the toilet. The only bright spark in the old folks' home was George the budgie. She was always happy.

So Brenda bought a budgie of her own and called it Clive. The trouble was that Clive didn't like Brenda. Every time she went near him, he would put his head on one side and swear like a very angry sailor. Brenda hadn't heard some of the words Clive said before but she got the general idea and gave Clive to the old people's home, where he taught George a lot of new words.

Norman became forty-two. He had read somewhere that forty-two was the meaning of life so he decided it was time for decisive action. He put a card in the corner shop's window.

ARTIST'S MODEL
Fifi La Strange

Lonely gentleman seeks partner in life, no fish or budgerigars.

0678 141519 after 6 p.m.

LOST
in West High Street
Friday morning
Brand New
Marmalade Sandw

Brenda became forty-two. She had read somewhere that forty-two was the meaning of life so she decided it was time for decisive action. She put a card in the corner shop's window.

FOR SALE
Marmalade
Sandwich
One
careful owner

Lonely lady seeks partner in life, no amphibians or budgerigars.

P.O. Box 23779a

ARTIST'S MODE
Amy Lissiat

He only got one reply. It was from a lady who said she was looking for a partner too, but could never fall in love with someone who hated animals.

The shop assistant was a sloppy girl and didn't use enough sticky tape. Brenda's card fell down a narrow gap behind the window sill, where it was eaten by ants.

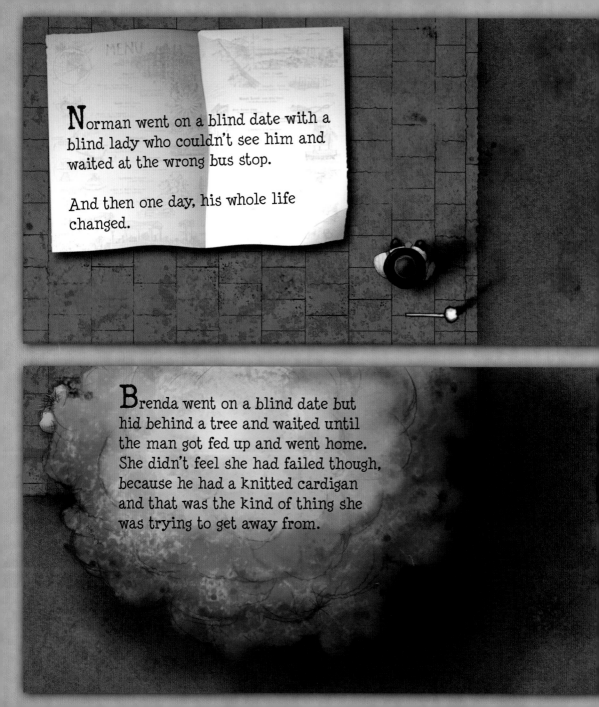

Norman went on a blind date with a blind lady who couldn't see him and waited at the wrong bus stop.

And then one day, his whole life changed.

Brenda went on a blind date but hid behind a tree and waited until the man got fed up and went home. She didn't feel she had failed though, because he had a knitted cardigan and that was the kind of thing she was trying to get away from.

And then one day, her whole life changed.

In order to avoid complications, Norman always looked at his shoes when he walked down the street.

Brenda had often wondered if the world would look any better from above. It had only been a casual thought, certainly not big enough to buy a ladder or go up in a hot air balloon. Besides, she didn't like hot air, it made her hair frizzy. But one day as she walked down the street, Brenda passed a ladder leaning against the side of a very tall building and decided to see if the world was actually any better from above.

She began to climb. Halfway up the world didn't look any better, just a bit smaller.

But one day, for no reason he could remember, Norman looked up, not just as high as other people's faces, but right up into the sky.

Further up it looked blurry too and Brenda got a funny feeling. She'd heard the word "vertigo" but never bothered with it. Now she wished she had.

Her head began to swim and her breakfast began to wonder if it wanted to stay inside her tummy or come back outside. The ladder seemed to have turned into jelly along with Brenda's legs. Then slowly and suddenly at the same time, the ladder and Brenda decided they didn't want to be together any more.

And that is how she landed on top of Norman.

HAPPINESS

Norman, who had cushioned Brenda's fall, had thirty-seven broken bones and was unconscious. Brenda, who had landed on a nice soft Norman, only broke nine quite small bones and wasn't. She was up and about in less than a week. Every day she went and sat by Norman's bed and realized that she was falling deeply in love. Norman, still unconscious, had dreams of being squashed by a quite large bottom wearing a tweed skirt.

They were both happier than they had ever been before.

Norman woke up and looked at Brenda. She was holding his hand. No one had ever done that before. She said she was sorry she fell on him and he said it was all right, he hadn't been going anywhere special. She said Norman had saved her life and he said he was glad because if she had been dead she wouldn't be holding his hand and he quite liked it.

One thing led to a whole lot of others. Norman and Brenda got married and lived happily ever after with no aquatic creatures or budgerigars.

Which simply goes to show that even if you spend a lot of your life washing up at parties or talking to goldfish, somewhere in the world there is someone just for you.

You simply have to be in the right place at the right time.

The Normans and Brendas never start wars.

Kane/Miller Book Publishers, Inc.
First American Edition 2009
by Kane/Miller Book Publishers, Inc.
La Jolla, California

Originally published in Australia by Lothian Books,
an imprint of Hachette Children's Books Australia, 2006

Kane/Miller Book Publishers, Inc.
P.O. Box 8515
La Jolla, CA 92038
www.kanemiller.com

Library of Congress Control Number: 2008932210

ISBN: 978-1-933605-86-9
Printed and bound in China
1 2 3 4 5 6 7 8 9 10

Designed by Colin Thompson
Illustration technique:
Photoshop on an Apple Macintosh